Belle

The Brave Princess

Retold by **Amelia Hansen** · Illustrated by **Angel Rodríguez**

Autumn
Publishing

Once upon a time, an old woman came to the castle of a spoilt and selfish prince. She offered him a single rose in exchange for shelter, but the Prince turned her away.

The old woman was really **an enchantress!**

She cast a spell on the castle.

Unless the Prince could learn to love – and earn someone's love

in return – before the rose's last petal fell, he would remain

**a beast
forever.**

Not far away, Belle dreamed of having

adventures

like those in her favourite books.

Gaston wanted
to marry Belle
because she was so
beautiful.

Gaston was handsome...

... but he was **very vain.**

Belle wanted

nothing

to do with him.

One day, Belle's father, **Maurice**,

set out for the fair with his new invention.

"**Goodbye, Papa!**" Belle called.

"**Good luck!**"

But soon Maurice became **lost** in the woods.

His horse, **Philippe**,

got scared and ran away.

And then wolves

attacked!

Frightened, Maurice

escaped

to a nearby castle.

It was the **Beast's castle!** Maurice was amazed by the enchanted servants. Lumiere and Mrs Potts welcomed him, but Cogsworth was worried the Beast would find out.

The Beast was **furious** to find a stranger in his home.

"So, you've come to stare at the Beast, have you?" he growled.

The Beast locked Maurice in the **dungeon**.

When Philippe returned alone,
Belle knew something **awful** had happened.
She rode off at once to find her father.

When Belle arrived at the castle, the Beast refused to let Maurice go. Belle looked up at the Beast **bravely**.

"Take me, instead," she said.

"You must promise to stay here forever," the Beast warned.

Belle was terrified, but she had to save her father.

"You have my word,"

replied Belle.

While Mrs Potts and Chip tried to **cheer** Belle up...

... the servants urged the Beast to be **gentle** with their new guest.

But he kept losing his **temper!**

That night, Belle discovered the enchanted **rose.**

The Beast cried out in **anger** when Belle tried to touch the rose. Terrified, Belle fled from the castle.

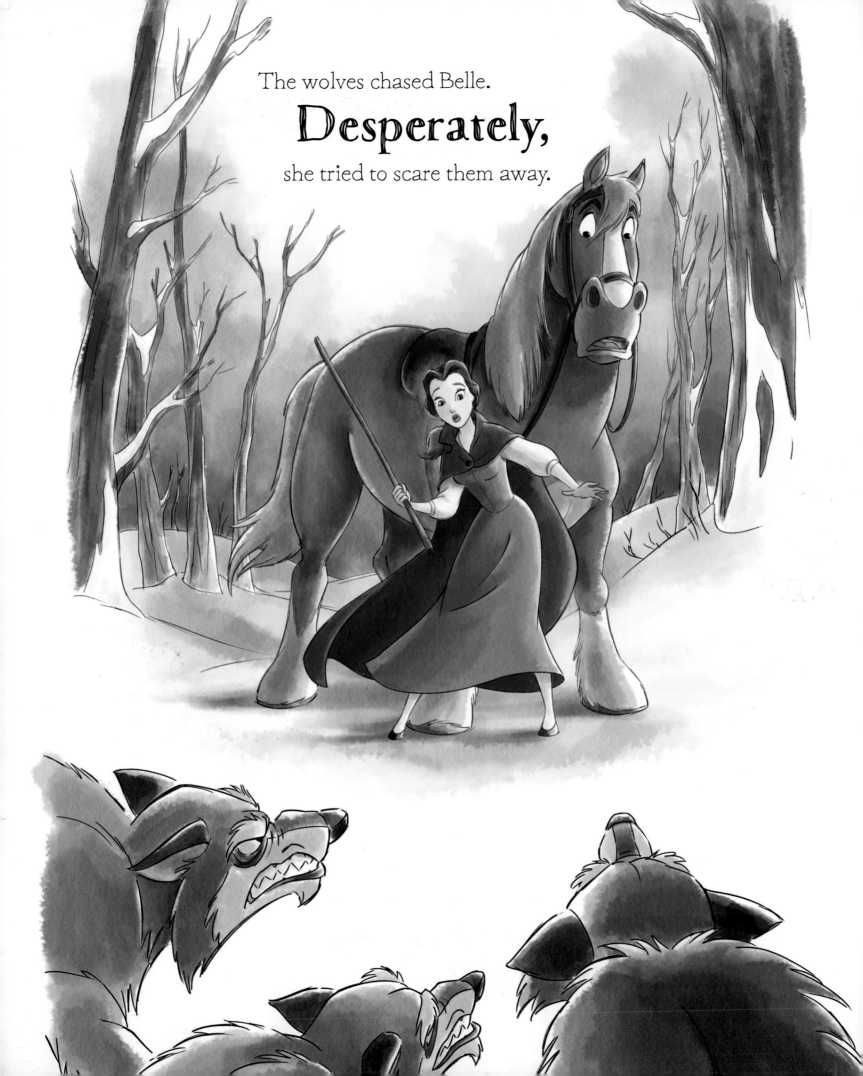

The wolves chased Belle.
Desperately,
she tried to scare them away.

Then the Beast appeared! He **fought**

off the wolves, but they hurt him.

Belle wanted to leave,

but she knew the Beast needed

her **help.**

Back at the castle, Belle thanked the Beast for

saving her life.

"You're welcome," he replied.

They started to get along better after that.

One evening, the Beast
invited Belle to
a **special** dinner.

Belle was **excited.**

The Wardrobe helped her
to choose the perfect outfit,
a **beautiful** golden ball gown
with matching gloves and shoes.

The Beast was on his very best behaviour at dinner. When the music started, Belle pulled him into the ballroom to dance with her. The Beast knew he had **fallen in love.**

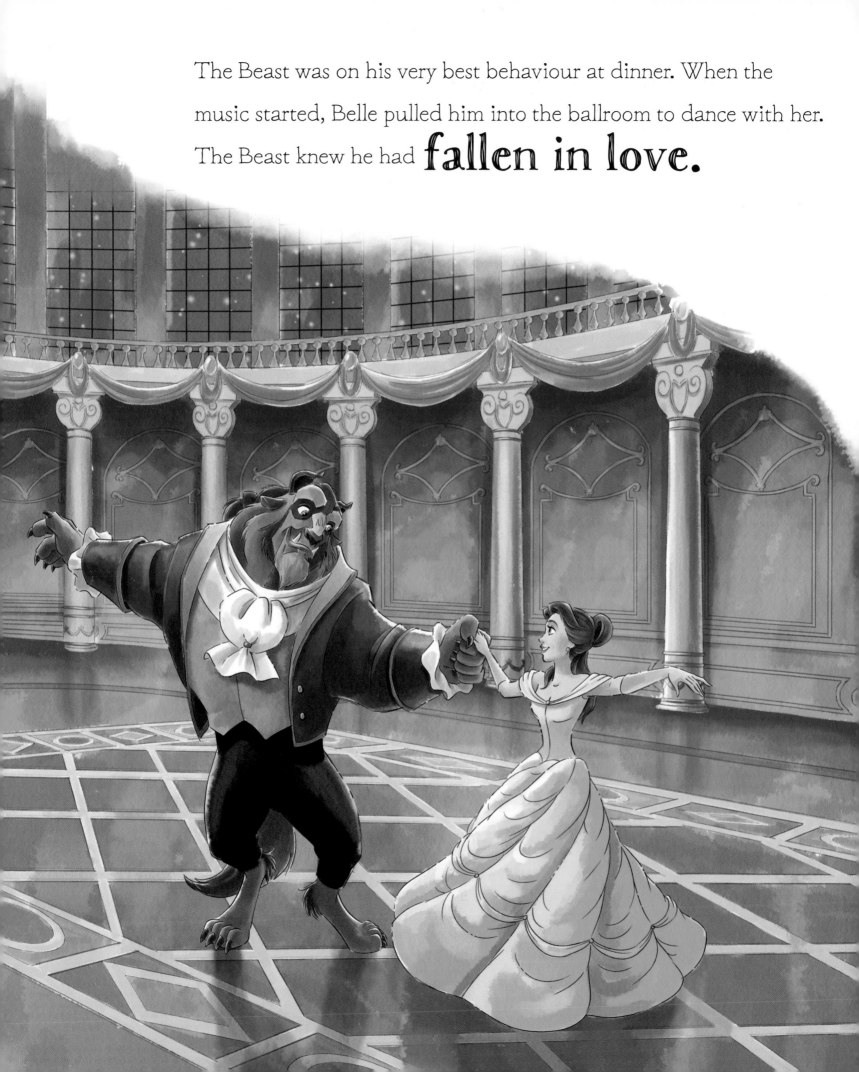

The Beast let Belle use his magic mirror

to see her father. It showed Maurice in

trouble!

"Then you must go to him," the Beast told Belle.

By setting his true love free, he lost any hope of

breaking his curse.

He gave her the mirror so she would always

remember him.

At home, Maurice was overjoyed to see Belle, but soon there was a knock at the door. Maurice had been telling stories about the Beast and the villagers thought he was **crazy**.
They had come to take him away!

"My father's not crazy!" Belle said. She showed

them the Beast in the mirror. Gaston convinced the others that

the Beast was **dangerous.** He led them towards

the castle to kill the Beast!

Belle was devastated. She had to warn her **friend!**

Belle and her father raced off as fast as they could.

Gaston was the first to arrive at the castle. **He attacked,** but the Beast didn't fight back. With Belle no longer in his life, nothing seemed to matter to the Beast.

"No!" shouted Belle, seeing the struggle. When the Beast heard Belle's voice, his strength returned. He grabbed Gaston and whispered, **"Get out."**

But when the Beast turned to Belle,
Gaston stabbed him in the back! The Beast
roared in pain. Startled, Gaston
fell to the rocks below.

Belle pulled the Beast to safety, but he was badly hurt.

"Please don't leave me," Belle said, sobbing.

"I love you."

With those three words, the **spell** was broken!

Belle stared as the Beast **transformed** into a handsome, human prince.

Happy cries rang out as the servants **turned back** into humans.
But no one was more **joyful** than Belle and her prince.

And, of course, they lived
happily ever after.